D0975406

TOY ACADEMY

SOME ASSEMBLY REQUIRED

BRIAN LYNCH
ILLUSTRATED BY EDWARDIAN TAYLOR

SCHOLASTIC PRESS
NEW YORK

For Henry, my best buddy, my greatest [co]creation —B.L.

To Jamey and my mini wolf pack: Samurai, Hansel, and Jinx. —E.T.

• • •

All rights reserved. Published by Scholastic Press, an imprint of
Scholastic Inc., *Publishers since 1920*. SCHOLASTIC, SCHOLASTIC PRESS,
and associated logos are trademarks and/or registered trademarks
of Scholastic Inc.

The publisher does not have any control over and does not assume
any responsibility for author or third-party websites or their content.

Library of Congress Cataloging-in-Publication Data available

ISBN 978-1-338-14845-9

10 9 8 7 6 5 4 3 2 1   18 19 20 21 22

Printed in the U.S.A.   23
First edition, February, 2018

Book design by Mary Claire Cruz

CHAPTER ONE
TOY MEETS WORLD

The small toy sat up in the garbage can and smiled. He had been alive a whole minute so far, and things were going great. He already had a place to stay and half a waffle if he got hungry.

Under the waffle, there was a used doll pattern from the **U CAN SEW** company. And under *that* was the first attempt at a very angry letter.

Dear U CAN SEW,

My name is Gertrude Konikoff. I am eight years old and I am fantastic at sewing. I have ~~pree previsually~~ previously made a scarf and quilt and part of a sweater. So when I saw that your stuffed animal pattern was for "advanced sewers," I said great, that's what I am. Well, let me tell you, this was too hard and it came out all weird. I gave him a name (Grumbolt) and tried playing with him and everything. But he is simply unplayable. His arms are different lengths, his head is too big for his body, and he has a ~~ludicriss ridic~~ goofy look on his face. I demand my money back and an apology. I mean business.

Wow, did he feel bad for whatever doll that girl was insulting.

But the note had given him an idea. He should find a kid to call his own.

Figuring that kid was *not* going to be in the garbage can, he reached up to the rim to pull himself out—and saw that his arms were two different lengths.

No, it couldn't be.

Just to be sure, he felt his head. Sure enough, it was oversized.

He was the stuffed animal in the letter!

He didn't appreciate his face being called "goofy," but at least he now knew his name: **GRUMBOLT**. It was the best name he had ever heard. (That said, he had only heard two names his whole life, and the other belonged to the girl who threw him in the garbage can.)

Grumbolt climbed out and slid down the side into a nice, quiet kitchen. As soon as his feet hit the tile floor, Grumbolt noticed something on the refrigerator: his reflection. He had never seen himself before and wanted to take a look.

Grumbolt heard a steady hum from behind, and a shadow fell over him. He turned around and found himself face-to-giant-face with Gertrude's cat. Grumbolt waved excitedly. "Hello! Do you want to play?"

The large beast studied the little doll. Grumbolt was small, and he was moving. First law of cat logic:

SMALL
+
MOVING
=
WANT TO EAT IT

The cat reeled back, hissed at her prey, and pounced.

CHAPTER TWO
SAND'S END

Grumbolt burst through the doggy door into the backyard. The cat was close behind.

"You don't want to hurt me," Grumbolt reasoned. "We're practically twins! Look, one of my ears is kinda catlike." Grumbolt paused. *Wow, could it be that he was a cat?*

The Beast didn't seem to care. She raised her claw to strike.

Grumbolt's eyes clenched shut. This was it; he had no regrets. Except for leaving his nice, safe garbage can. And starting a conversation with the cat. And not running faster. Okay, Grumbolt had many, many regrets.

But then the cat stopped.

She had spotted an orange butter-fly. It was smaller than Grumbolt, and moving faster. Second law of cat logic:

**SMALLER
+ MOVING FASTER =**

**WANT TO EAT IT
MORE**

The cat leaped over Grumbolt, chasing after her new prey.

He was safe and sound, and free to resume his mission: finding a kid to call his own.

Coincidentally, there was one playing next door.

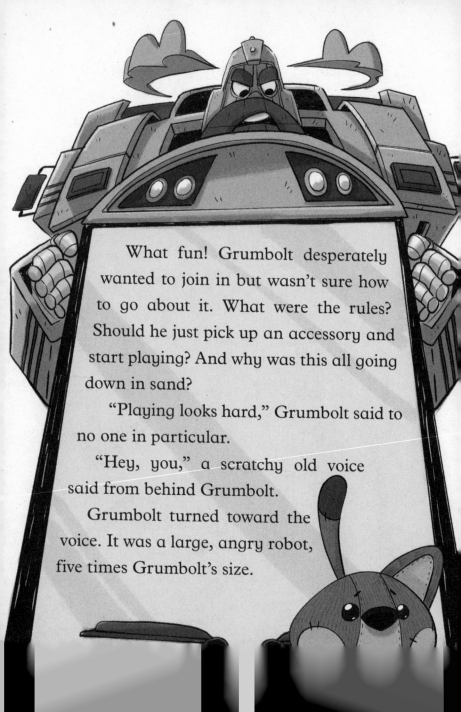

What fun! Grumbolt desperately wanted to join in but wasn't sure how to go about it. What were the rules? Should he just pick up an accessory and start playing? And why was this all going down in sand?

"Playing looks hard," Grumbolt said to no one in particular.

"Hey, you," a scratchy old voice said from behind Grumbolt.

Grumbolt turned toward the voice. It was a large, angry robot, five times Grumbolt's size.

CHAPTER THREE
BOT HERE'S THE THING

The old robot's colors were faded, his stickers yellowed and dirty. He had probably been, at one point, a cool-looking toy. He was not that anymore.

"Have you seen an armored panda?" the old robot asked.

"I don't think so," Grumbolt said to his new friend. "I'm—"

"There he is! Look, I don't have time to talk to you," the robot said. "I was supposed to be here *before* little Thomas over there opened his new action figures! That armored panda isn't ready. His box says he's the best fighter on the team, but he's terrible at play battle—"

Grumbolt turned, just as the armored panda failed to duck and his head went flying.

"You see?" The old robot sighed. "It was my job to go and get that panda and bring him to Toy Academy, but I was too busy talking to *you*."

"Excuse me, sir," Grumbolt said. "Did you say Toy Academy?"

"Yeah, I represent Commander Hedgehog's Institute for Novelty Academia," the robot barked. "The students call it Toy Academy."

"Yes, of course," Grumbolt said, but his face gave him away.

"You've never heard of it," the robot stated. "The academy's mission is to help toys learn how to play. You go to the school, you graduate, you receive the highly coveted **MADE IN CHINA** stamp." He lifted up his foot and showed Grumbolt the stamp on the bottom. "**CHINA:** short for **COMMANDER HEDGEHOG'S INSTITUTE FOR NOVELTY ACADEMIA.** Classes start *tomorrow*, and that panda was a prime candidate for Toy Academy. But, at the very least, you gotta have a head."

Grumbolt perked up. *He* had a head. Some had argued that he had *too much* of a head. He smiled winningly at the old robot.

"Get that look off your face," the robot snapped.

"I can't. It's my go-to look. It's the one Gertrude sewed on my face. Sir, Mr. . . . ?"

"**OMNIBUS SQUARED**," the robot shot back.

"Mr. OmniBus, sir, I'm a very new toy." Grumbolt puffed out his chest. "I need to learn. So if I went to Toy Academy and was really good . . ."

OmniBus relented. "Then Child Placement Division would set you up with the perfect kid. That's *if* there's a kid out there for you. But I can't just *take* you to Toy Academy."

"Sure you can. You're out one armored panda. There's a space available," Grumbolt said, really hoping OmniBus didn't turn around and see the panda had put his head back on.

OmniBus had to admit that Grumbolt had a point. "Fine." He sighed. "Let's go."

His waist spun 180 degrees. His arms retracted into his body. A set of wheels descended from his underbelly. OmniBus was transforming right before Grumbolt's eyes!

CHAPTER FOUR
MICROMANAGED

The transformation was taking a very long time. OmniBus wasn't as sharp as he used to be, and transforming was a complicated process.

OmniBus eventually managed to turn himself into a school bus. He opened his doors and Grumbolt climbed in. The bus sped down the sidewalk.

"OmniBus, sir, is Toy Academy nearby, please?"

OmniBus's voice came over the bus radio. "We have a stop to make first. Gotta pick up another student."

OmniBus parked in an alley next to a store called Earth Prime Comics and Toys. Waiting next to the back door was a small action figure. She was very well painted and very well made. She was also wrapped in a protective bag.

"Are you Micro?" OmniBus boomed.

"Yes, sir," the action figure responded. "And are you a 1984 first-edition OmniBus Squared?"

"Yep," OmniBus said, letting her aboard.

Micro high-fived herself.

"How did you know that?" Grumbolt asked.

"I'm a little bit of a toy historian," the figure explained as she sat down. "I'm **MICRO GIGANTIC**."

"Grumbolt," Grumbolt said, putting his paw out. "I'm a little bit of a toy."

Micro did her best to shake, but the plastic wrapping made it quite awkward.

"Sorry." Micro sighed.

"If you don't mind me asking—" Grumbolt started.

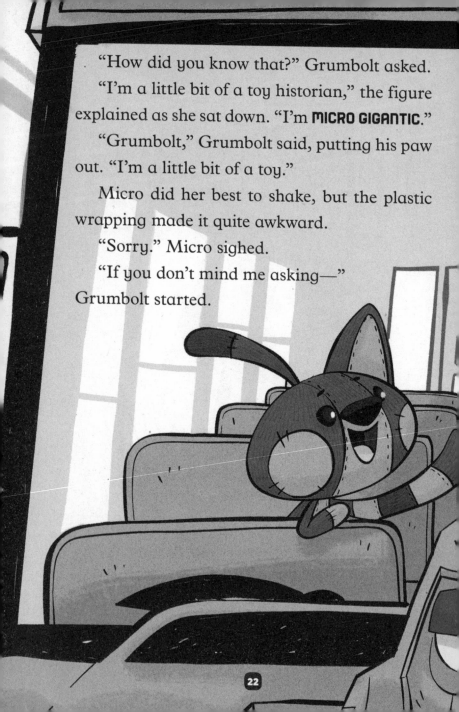

"The bag protects my value," Micro explained. "I'm a mail-away toy, super-rare and collectible. Eventually, I'll wind up on someone's shelf. Posing, inspiring, being admired."

"You don't want to play?" Grumbolt said.

"And get scratched? No. I plan to graduate in perfect condition."

"Now, if I can ask a question," Micro said. "What are you?"

Grumbolt shrugged. "I'm pretty sure I'm rare, too. I mean, Gertrude only made one of me."

"Yes, but **WHAT ARE YOU**?" Micro asked. "You look like a sea otter from one angle, but then you turn your head and you give off more of a woodchuck vibe."

"I'm not sure exactly what I am, not yet," Grumbolt said. "I only know I'm gonna be the best toy ever."

At that moment, OmniBus was rapidly approaching their destination. And it was **INCREDIBLE**.

24

CHAPTER FIVE
IN THE ZONE

The bus drove right up to the toy store's automatic doors, just as an employee ran in late for work. The automatic door slid open, and OmniBus zipped through, speeding past the cash registers before anyone noticed him.

OmniBus turned a corner, taking a shortcut through an aisle filled with hundreds of boxes containing dolls clad in polka dots. Her

name was Margie and there was one for every occasion!

"She's incredible!" Grumbolt exclaimed.

Micro nodded. "She's the most popular doll in the world. Created in 1954 in Carmel, Indiana, there are 4,000 different kinds of Margies and at least 45,602 clothing and/or uniform options."

"You have so many facts in your head!" Grumbolt gasped, impressed. "I just have gobs of cotton."

OmniBus zoomed straight to the discount section. This was the dumping ground for all the unpopular toys. They sat depressed in their dusty boxes, their hopes and dreams of being someone's prized possession long since forgotten. There was something called **VEGGIE WARRIORS** that was supposed to be the next big toy, but that absolutely no one had bought. Something called **MY FIRST SNAIL FARM** that was no one's first anything.

Grumbolt was sad to see all these toys without any kids to play with. He made a promise to himself: No matter how hard Toy Academy was, he was going to pass. He was going to get great at playing. He was going to get himself a **KID**. He was *not* going to end up like a Veggie Warrior.

On the floor of the discount section was a giant playset called **WARP ZONE**. OmniBus picked up speed, hurtling right toward it.

"Uh, OmniBus, you're about to drive right into that t-toy," Grumbolt stammered. Micro started blowing into her bag, trying to create an airbag to soften the impact.

OmniBus barked into his speaker box, **"INCOMING, SVEN!"**

An action figure sitting on top of Warp Zone pulled a lever, revealing a plastic tunnel. In the center of the tunnel was a cardboard dial that was spinning.

IT SPUN FASTER AND FASTER...

...AND OMNIBUS SAILED THROUGH IT.

The entire bus was bathed in light, and then disappeared. Grumbolt was no longer in the toy store. He was no longer in the world he knew at all.

CHAPTER SIX
BRIGHT LIGHTS, SMALL CITY

OMNIBUS ROCKETED OUT OF THE TUNNEL AND INTO THE

TOY WORLD!

DIORAMA DESERT
PLAYVILLE
TOY TALK
e&j toys
EXIT
STOP

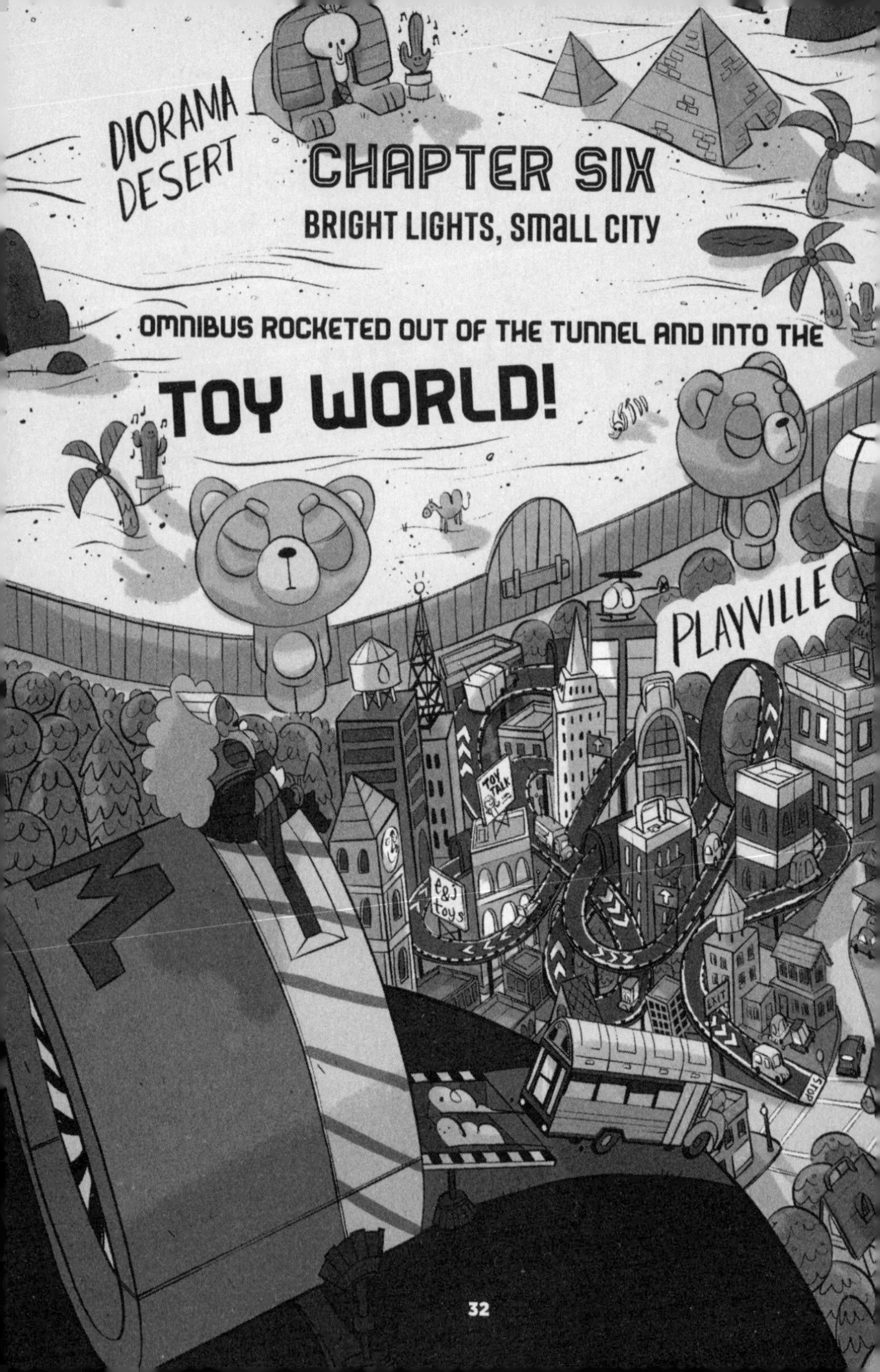

EVIL TOY ACADEMY

TOY ACADEMY

KNICKKNACK VALLEY

PLASTIC GROVE FARM LANDS

BAUBLE BAY

Eventually, the road split into two.

"What's that?" Grumbolt asked, a shiver running up where his spine should be. He pointed to a massive lair shaped like a skull, perched on top of a deserted mountain. The sky over the lair was pitch-black, illuminated every now and then by quick flashes of lightning.

"That is the **EVIL TOY ACADEMY**," Micro said. "Monsters, henchmen, lackeys . . . every villain from every toy line goes there. It was founded by Commander Hedgehog's archenemy, the despicable **CHANCELLOR THORNBONES**."

Luckily, OmniBus turned away at the last second. Ahead, Grumbolt could see a sprawling campus atop a sunny mountain, surrounded by super-high block gates.

"I can't believe we're here!" Micro gasped.

"Believe it," OmniBus proclaimed. "Micro, uh, Other Thing, **WELCOME TO TOY ACADEMY**."

ETA

TOY ACADEMY

CHAPTER SEVEN
FRESHMEN DISORIENTATION

Toy Academy was made up of the coolest playsets from every existing toy line.

Grumbolt and Micro joined the crowd of students streaming toward an incredible five-story castle in the center of campus.

"That's **CASTLE FORT LAIR**, Commander Hedgehog's headquarters!" Micro exclaimed. "I never thought I'd see one up close. Any kid who got a Castle Fort Lair for their birthday didn't ask for any other gifts for the next three holidays. They were still finding new, cool features in Castle Fort Lair: trapdoors, slides, bubble machines—Grumbolt, I'm going to pass out!"

Micro wasn't exaggerating. She was breathing so heavily her plastic bag was expanding in and out, threatening to pop.

"Micro, what's with those guys?" Grumbolt said, trying to distract her. He pointed to plastic robots patrolling Castle Fort Lair, eyeballing the students as they entered.

"Beat-Bots. Commander Hedgehog's security force," Micro explained, slightly calmer. "According to the minicomic that came with the playset, each Castle Fort Lair comes with 301 of them."

BEAT-BOTS CAN SCAN AN OPPONENT AND FIND THEIR WEAKNESS IN SECONDS

ICE DEMON...

WEAKNESS: FIRE!

A Beat-Bot rolled past Grumbolt and Micro.
A nervous Grumbolt smiled politely. He knew
they were there for his protection, but he really
didn't want to be scanned. Not even a little.

The students entered the castle, where the faculty and staff were waiting. These were older toys, their days of play behind them, here to pass their knowledge on to a new generation of plastic and cloth.

IRVING SPIDER-RING, a former goody-bag prize, informed the crowd that Commander Hedgehog would be here as soon as someone could find him. "Sometimes the commander likes to wander—"

All of a sudden, Commander Hedgehog sprung out from a trapdoor in the floor, nearly giving Irving a heart attack.

"And sometimes he likes to surprise the other faculty to keep them on their toes!" the commander bellowed.

The commander turned and faced the students. The paint on his uniform was faded and scratched. He didn't have much articulation. His right hip joint was glued into place. But he wore it well.

"Welcome to **COMMANDER HEDGEHOG'S INSTITUTE FOR NOVELTY ACADEMIA!**" the commander proclaimed. "Who's excited to be here?"

The students cheered enthusiastically, especially the toy next to Grumbolt. He was unable to contain his excitement, and Grumbolt could immediately see why this guy loved Commander Hedgehog so much. He was a *bootleg* Commander Hedgehog toy. Except for a few details, he was almost exactly like Commander Hedgehog.

Made from polyurethane (the flimsiest plastic)

Hot-pink paint job

Accessories consist of plunger and frying pan

BOOTLEG

Made from acrylonitrile butadiene styrene (the finest plastic)

Cool silver paint job

Accessories consist of space axe and star sword

THE REAL COMMANDER HEDGEHOG

The bootleg noticed Grumbolt looking at him.

"I know what you're thinking! But I'm not a bootleg," the bootleg said. "I'm an original toy who happens to be ever so slightly similar to Commander Hedgehog. My name is COMMANDANT HEDGEPIG."

Grumbolt nodded. "Okay. I'm Grumbolt."

"So, what are you supposed to be?"

Grumbolt shrugged.

Bootleg was the third person to question what Grumbolt was, a troubling fact as Grumbolt had, at this point, only talked to three people.

Grumbolt heard laughter from behind him. He turned, hoping for a change of subject and that he could be part of the fun.

But what he saw wasn't fun at all.

CHAPTER EIGHT
HERE GOES EVERYTHING

An army action figure was pointing and laughing at a ceramic boy and girl.

"You losers don't belong here! You aren't even toys!" the army man chortled. "You're salt-and-pepper shakers!"

He grabbed the ceramic boy and held him by the ankles, shaking him vigorously. Sure enough, salt poured out of three tiny holes in his head.

The boy flailed about helplessly as the army man happily declared, "Toys do NOT dispense seasoning! Ever! *I'm* a toy! I'm the best toy!"

"Doubtful," Grumbolt quietly whispered to Micro.

Everyone turned and stared at Grumbolt. The army man stopped in his tracks, glared at him, and growled, "What'd you say?"

Evidently, Grumbolt hadn't whispered it *that* quietly.

The army man dropped the salt shaker and marched right up to Grumbolt. "Listen, you space rodent—"

Grumbolt paused. *Hmmmm, maybe he was a space rodent.* That could be cool, and something to bond over with Commander Hedgehog.

"—I'M REX EVERYTHING. I lead Elite Action Force Now."

Grumbolt thought about it. "Not to nitpick, but no, you don't. Maybe someday you will, but right now you're just a student like us."

"I'm nothing like you!" Rex shouted. "I'm an interdimensional defender of freedom and all that is right. I encounter something bad, I give 'em a taste of my action feature. You wanna see it?"

"Move outta the way, mutant chipmunk!" the ceramic girl yelled to Grumbolt.

Rex tapped a button on his shoulder, making his right leg shoot forward with incredible spring action. It was a blur of plastic muscle that hit Grumbolt in the chest, sending him flying back onto the ground. Luckily, his big pillowy head cushioned the fall.

Rex laughed. "That's called the **REX-IN-EFFECT** kick. It's the greatest action feature ever, and I use it to strike down evil."

When Grumbolt tried to get up, Rex exclaimed, "Looks like someone wants another taste of my action feature!"

Rex was just about to tap his shoulder button a second time, when a tiny hand grabbed him by the arm, swung him into the air, and smashed him onto the ground. Commander Hedgehog stood before them. His army of Beat-Bots stood behind him, ready for action.

"You want to tangle, boys? Tangle with me," Commander Hedgehog said. "Though I warn you, *every* move I make is an action feature."

It was a bold statement. Made only slightly less bold by the fact that the commander's arm, loosened when he flipped Rex, fell off his shoulder and hit the ground.

"I really have to tighten these things," the commander muttered as he picked up his arm. "Listen, there is no fighting on campus. Whatsoever. Unless you're in Fighting 101, Fighting 201, Advanced Fighting, or Creative Fighting. You have started this school year off very badly, Rex Everything—"

He looked at Grumbolt.

"—and *whatever* you are."

Commander Hedgehog went back to the stage and resumed his speech.

Rex glared at Grumbolt. "This isn't over, you . . . dopey groundhog."

The ceramic sister helped Grumbolt up.

"Thank you. I'm **PEPPER SHAKER**," she said. "This is my brother, **SALT**."

Salt was trembling so hard that salt was spraying from his head. "We should have stayed on that old lady's dinner table, where it was safe."

"Don't listen to him." Pepper smiled.

Despite the ugliness of the last few moments, Grumbolt was happy to have two new friends.

"In summation," Commander Hedgehog said, "welcome to Toy Academy! Where anything can happen!"

Commander Hedgehog waved his hand over a symbol on the castle wall. The symbol lit up and the floor started moving! It spun them into a completely different room. They were now in the armory!

Bootleg turned to Grumbolt and excitedly explained, "Everything in the castle playset is activated by the Commander Hedgehog figure. He's the key! The commander's arms unlock cool weapons and hidden compartments! Even the bubble machine!"

"Rumor has it that Castle Fort Lair has a sno-cone maker," Micro added. "But I've never been able to confirm it."

"You will," Grumbolt said, patting her on the back of her bag.

After the welcome party, Grumbolt and friends reported to the freshmen dorms, which were actually Princess Dream Mansions that Margie, the most successful doll ever, had graciously donated. Luckily for Grumbolt, his roommate was Paper Dave, a very neat and tidy paper doll who kept to himself. In fact, at certain angles, Grumbolt didn't even know Paper Dave was in the room.

Grumbolt laid on his M-shaped bed (Margie loved the letter *M*) and adjusted his polka-dot pillow (Margie loved polka dots even more than the letter *M*) and closed his eyes. Today could have gone better. But tomorrow he'd turn it all around. Tomorrow he'd begin his education and prove to everyone that he was the very best toy in the world.

CHAPTER NINE
MAJOR DILEMMA

The next morning, Grumbolt met with his guidance counselor, Irving Spider-Ring, to find out what classes he'd be taking. There were many different majors at the school to help toys concentrate on becoming the best toy they could be.

EDUCATION

EDUCATIONAL TOYS TEACH KIDS SPELLING, MATH, YOU NAME IT! EVERYONE LOVES TO LEARN!

TIE-BOT, THE ROBOT WHO CAN TIE HIS OWN SHOES

SEE-THRU SAM AND HIS VISIBLE GUTS

LEARN SPANISH MARGIE

This piqued Grumbolt's interest. He'd love to share his knowledge with children. He felt he had learned a lot in the twenty-four hours he had been alive.

COLLECTIBLE

STATUES! RARE TOYS! SIT ON A SHELF AND BRING JOY TO EVERYONE WHO SEES YOU!

TIN ROCKET TOY

"WORLD'S FANCIEST SWIMMER" STATUE

MARGIE SUPERHERO STATUE

Grumbolt thought about it. There was only ONE of him; that meant he was rare. But collectibles didn't get to play, and that's what Grumbolt really wanted to do.

ACTION

OUR MOST POPULAR MAJOR! LEARN HOW TO BATTLE, GO ON QUESTS, AND, WHEN NECESSARY, SAVE THE WORLD!

COMMANDER HEDGEHOG

REX EVERYTHING AND HIS ELITE ACTION FORCE NOW

LASER ATTACK MARGIE

Grumbolt smiled big; this sounded cool. This was a good fit. Grumbolt was **DEFINITELY** an action figure.

"Grumbolt," Irving Spider-Ring said. "You are *definitely* a plush."

PLUSHES

CUDDLY DOLLS OF THE WORLD, GET READY TO SOOTHE, COMFORT, AND TAKE LOTS AND LOTS AND LOTS OF NAPS!

STUFFIES

BABY CRIES-A-LOT

WEIRD, HANDMADE MYSTERY ANIMALS

"You're gonna get hugged a lot," Irving declared. "You're a little small to hug, but we'll just find you a really small child."

"Fantastic!" Grumbolt said. "Though, one arm is shorter than the other, so any return hugging might prove difficult. Is that going to be a problem?"

Irving shrugged. "Probably! Have a great first day!"

CHAPTER TEN
PLUSH LIFE

First period was Tea Parties 101, and Grumbolt's teacher was T4-2. Rumor had it he was programmed by NASA to be the best tea party guest of all time.

"By the time you finish my class," T4-2 proclaimed, "you will be ready for any tea party, thrown by any child, in any situation. Let's begin with basic tea party etiquette. Any volunteers?"

Grumbolt jumped up and volunteered. He was raring to go. T4-2 handed him a teacup.

"I am a six-year-old girl who is scared of the dark, wants to be president when she grows up, and is allergic to fish," T4-2 said. "Commence tea party."

This was it! Grumbolt was finally about to play. His lucky classmates would be the first to see history being made. Word of his super-toy status would spread throughout school. By lunch, he'd be a legend. By the end of the week, the school would want to build a statue of him, but Grumbolt would refuse. (He was humble, after all.) He'd be so good he'd zip through all four years of classes in a month. A month after *that*, he'd have a kid of his own.

He raised the cup of invisible tea to his mouth, sipped it, and stated, "Mmmm, this is stellar tea."

Great start. Maybe the best.

T4-2 leaned in and asked, "What are you?"

Grumbolt stared back at his teacher.

"I mean," T4-2 said, "what kind of animal are you?"

Grumbolt had no response. Was T4-2 asking as the future-president girl who was allergic to fish, or was his teacher so perplexed by Grumbolt's appearance that he broke character?

"W-what does it matter?" Grumbolt stammered. "What are *you* is a better question."

"Never get angry with your child," T4-2 said calmly. "You have just made her cry. Word will spread throughout the neighborhood. You will not be invited back to her tea party. You will be banned from tea-related get-togethers for years to come."

Grumbolt slumped back in his chair.

Second period was Introduction to Dress-Up. The students met in a classroom packed with all sorts of toy fashions. They waited for their teacher to arrive.

They waited and waited and waited.

A stuffed horse was starting to get annoyed. "Where *is* our teacher?"

"She's right here!" the chair under the horse responded. The horse screamed as the chair started moving.

"Your teacher was in the room the entire time!" a pig in a black turtleneck announced, shedding her chair costume. "I'm **DRAMA PIG,**

and you've just learned your first lesson in the art of dress-up!"

The entire class applauded. The stuffed horse was a little weirded out.

"The right clothes can change **ANYONE!**" Drama Pig declared. "Take this guy," she said, passing a stuffed worm. "One hat later . . ."

Drama Pig plopped a baseball hat on the worm's head.

"Wow!" the worm declared. "Now I'm an all-star athlete!"

Drama Pig strutted past a leathery lizard doll. "And what about this scaly monster?"

The leathery lizard looked sad, until Drama Pig tossed a frilly hat atop his head.

"Whoa!" Leathery Lizard exclaimed. "Now I'm a high-society debutant!"

Drama Pig turned to the class. "Your first assignment . . . become a cowboy. You have one minute."

The class rushed to the piles of clothes and grabbed any cowboy hat or boots they could find. There were cowboy worms and cowboy lizards and cowboy cows.

Grumbolt found a sweet ten-gallon hat. He put it on and looked in the mirror. Yes, he looked like a supercool cowboy all right.

He looked again. Did he look like a cowboy, or some kind of dressed-up space rodent? Would everyone else just see some mystery animal in a big hat?

As Drama Pig walked up to each student and graded his or her cowboy looks, Grumbolt knew he had to do something. In a last-ditch attempt to pull off a look, he threw a sheet over his body, and then placed the cowboy hat on top of that.

"Uh, I'm a cowboy ghost," Grumbolt said.

Grumbolt couldn't see Drama Pig's reaction. But he did hear Drama Pig's very loud sigh. Second period had gone even worse than the first.

Grumbolt's third class was Bedtime Prep, taught by Professor Cupcake Pillow. She had the most soothing voice Grumbolt had ever heard. With pretty, calming music playing in the background (full of violins, pianos, and gentle rain), the professor instructed her class on how to help settle their kids down before bed.

"Start with a bedtime story," Professor Cupcake Pillow said. Her sweet, melodic voice was like a thousand feathers tickling Grumbolt's ears.

"Be sure to keep the bedtime stories adventurous, lest you get them too mellow, nothing too adventurous, lest you get them too excited. For instance, I find the bedtime stories that are most effective think of sleep..."

Professor Cupcake Pillow looked out at the classroom. Her entire class was asleep. She used the rest of period to check her email.

Meanwhile, Micro was enjoying her school day. She was a collectible major and was assigned classes like Beginner's Dust Repelling and Living in a Box. There was only one problem: Her protective bag made it impossible to take notes. It was hard to grip a pen through the plastic. She considered asking other students if she could borrow their notes, but quite frankly, none of the students were *that good* at taking notes. Looking over Paper Dave's shoulder as he scribbled, she saw things like:

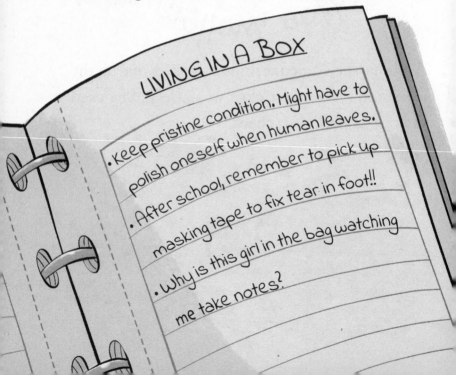

LIVING IN A BOX

• keep pristine condition. Might have to polish oneself when human leaves.

• After school, remember to pick up masking tape to fix tear in foot!!

• why is this girl in the bag watching me take notes?

But there was nothing Micro could do, short of ripping through the plastic bag and writing notes herself. *It's fine*, she told herself. She'd simply remember everything the teachers said.

Micro's third class of the day, Posing, didn't require writing. It just required her to hold poses for hours on end. She was very good at this.

"This is so fun!" Micro said.

"No, it's not!" Pepper shouted back. Turns out, Pepper and Salt were somewhat rare condiment dispensers, and they too were collectibles. "Posing is boring, and the changing weather simulations are just annoying."

SO FAR THEY HAD POSED IN A HAILSTORM,

IN A BLIZZARD,

IN A MONSOON,

AND DURING AN EARTHQUAKE.

Pepper broke her pose and sat down.

"I did my time standing still for thousands of dinners on that old lady's table!" Pepper exclaimed. "I want to play! I'm a toy!"

"You're not *just* a toy!" Micro cheered. "You're a collectible!"

Gym was the last class of the day. As Grumbolt waited for his teacher to arrive, he watched the action majors across the gymnasium. Rex Everything ran accessory battle drills with Bootleg. Bootleg's hands were molded, so he could only grasp the accessories he came packaged with. His plunger and pan were no match for Rex Everything's sword and nunchakus.

Grumbolt thought sparring looked superfun. But the stuffed horse informed him that plushes aren't taught to fight.

That's when OmniBus Squared stomped up to them. "The gym teacher for the plushes, Fanny Bunny, has retired. I'm your sub." He tossed pillows to each of the students.

"General rule of thumb is that plushes are just for hugging and cuddling," OmniBus sneered.

"But let me tell you something, when your kid runs at you with a pillow, he doesn't want to have a pillow **CUDDLE**, he wants to have a pillow **FIGHT**." OmniBus swung his pillow at the stuffed horse. **WHACK!** The horse fell to the floor.

OmniBus eyed Grumbolt and moved in. Grumbolt held his pillow tight, ready for action.

"And when it's late at night and your kid sends you under the bed because he or she

heard a noise, you think you're gonna beat the boogeyman by hugging him?" OmniBus asked Grumbolt.

"No way! I'm gonna fight!" Grumbolt shouted.

This was it! Grumbolt was going to hold his own with OmniBus Squared and prove that no matter what he was, he deserved to be at Toy Academy.

It was a good plan.

It was not to be.

Grumbolt's uneven arms made it impossible to swing the pillow with any kind of force. The old robot easily avoided Grumbolt's awkward pillow-flail before pillow-smashing Grumbolt and sending him to the ground.

CHAPTER ELEVEN
A FAREWELL TO ARM

Each passing day got tougher and tougher. More homework, more obstacles, more pillow combat. And Grumbolt had yet to complete a successful tea party. But he wasn't giving up. He practiced, he played, and he studied every night, usually falling asleep with a textbook in his paws.

Early one morning, he woke to the sound of a loud screeching alarm.

"What IS that?" Grumbolt said, springing out of bed.

The door flew open. It was one of Commander Hedgehog's Beat-Bots.

"Report to Castle Fort Lair immediately," the Beat-Bot commanded. "Commander Hedgehog's left arm has been stolen."

Everyone on campus assembled at Castle Fort Lair. Commander Hedgehog, sure enough, was down to one arm. He explained to the crowd that while he slept, someone had snuck into his bedroom and swiped it.

"There was a time when I would have heard this coming," he said, his voice sad and low. "Getting older makes you more valuable on eBay, but less valuable in life."

An extremely distraught Bootleg raised his hand up into the air. "Take my arm! It's so similar!"

"Nobody wants your dumb pink arms, Bootleg," Rex said. "Why would anyone want to hold a plunger all the time?"

Commander Hedgehog didn't want Bootleg's arm. The only arms Commander Hedgehog wanted were his own.

"My arms unlock everything in Castle Fort Lair. Without old lefty, I can't access half the secret features. No bubble machines, no revolving floor . . ."

"We all know who stole them," OmniBus growled.

The commander nodded and waved his remaining hand over a keypad on the wall. A plastic television screen lowered from the ceiling. He tapped a few buttons on the keypad below and said, "Adventure-Screen, please call . . . the Evil Toy Academy."

The Adventure-Screen patched through to the Evil Toy Academy, and Grumbolt got his first look at the sinister Chancellor Thornbones, Commander Hedgehog's arch nemesis and the founder of Evil Toy Academy.

"Oh, Commander Hedgehog! What a *wonderful* surprise to hear from you!" Thornbones cackled. His high-pitched voice scraped the inside of Grumbolt's ears.

"Knock it off, Thornbones," the commander insisted. "Give me my arm back!"

"You're missing an arm?" Thornbones said, leaning in to get a better look. "Oh yes, now I see it. Well, that's terrible. Commander, we've had our differences, but you must know I would never take a limb; that would be underhanded. Pardon the pun. Because you're missing a hand, you see."

The commander pounded the monitor. "Give me my arm back!"

"Don't yell at me!" Thornbones screeched. He smacked a button, ending the call.

"Don't you worry, Commander. I'm gonna drive down to Evil Toy Academy and get your arm back!" OmniBus shouted. "And maybe for good measure, I'll take a couple of theirs."

"I appreciate that, old friend." The commander sighed. "But that would just bring more trouble. Besides, you'd never get by the **GUARD BURGER**."

"The Guard Burger." OmniBus gulped. "I thought he was just a myth."

If the commander's arm *was* at the Evil Toy Academy, it looked like it was going to stay there.

Commander Hedgehog turned and faced the students.

"All of you, please be careful," Commander Hedgehog said. "If they were able to get on campus, they might have hidden a spy among us. Someone in this school might be evil. It could be a teacher, or a classmate. Heck, your roommate could be plotting the school's very destruction."

A hush fell over the room.

"Well, sleep tight!"

CHAPTER TWELVE
TEA PARTY CRASHER

Tensions were running high. Beat-Bots patrolled the campus day and night. The faculty was on edge. And the students didn't know whom to trust.

"If there's a villain on campus, I'm gonna find him!" Rex Everything declared in gym class. "Though maybe Commander Hedgehog should take this as a sign and retire."

"And just *who* could possibly take over?" Bootleg snapped.

"That's not for me to say," Rex said. "But it should be someone smart and tough, with a secret kick that's activated by tapping my shoulder."

Grumbolt, meanwhile, was having his own trouble. He was failing Introduction to Dress-Up for lack of originality.

ASSIGNMENT:
DRESS AS ROYALTY.

ASSIGNMENT:
DRESS AS A PIRATE.

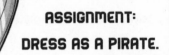

ASSIGNMENT:
DRESS AS A SCARY MONSTER.

And he STILL hadn't made it through Bedtime Prep without falling asleep, thanks to Professor Cupcake Pillow's dreamy voice. One day, as he was drifting off, he noticed something strange: a coat rack next to the door. It was strange because:

1. IT WASN'T THERE YESTERDAY.
2. THERE WAS A TELESCOPE PEEKING OUT FROM THE COATS.
3. IT SOUNDED LIKE THE COAT RACK HAD STARTED TO SNORE.

Grumbolt dozed off before he could say anything. When he woke up, the coat rack was gone.

It returned during gym. The same one, with the same telescope. Grumbolt was about to say something, when he was distracted by a few students talking about him. Whispering, pointing. He leaned in to get a better listen. One of the dolls immediately realized this and turned down her volume knob so Grumbolt couldn't hear her. When he turned his attention back to the coat rack, it was gone.

Things got even weirder the next day in Tea Parties 101. Grumbolt was running tea party drills with T4-2.

"Your child is the youngest of eight children and is afraid of sudden movements," Grumbolt's teacher said. But Grumbolt wasn't listening because this room also had a new coat rack and this coat rack **ALSO HAD A TELESCOPE**. Grumbolt jumped up from the table, clutching his cup of invisible tea, causing T4-2 to proclaim, "Aaaah, sudden movement! Tea party fail!"

Grumbolt marched right up to the coat rack and tossed the contents of the teacup onto it.

Rex Everything fell out from under the coats! His face was covered in hot, invisible tea!

"Ow!" Rex proclaimed. "My perfectly molded face!"

"Why are you spying on us?" Grumbolt demanded.

"I'm not spying on everyone! I'm just spying on *you*!" Rex declared. "You stole the commander's arm!"

Grumbolt laughed it off; Rex wasn't making any sense. But no one else in the class was laughing. No one was coming to Grumbolt's defense. In fact, from the looks on their faces, they sided with Rex. That's what they must have been whispering about. **GRUMBOLT WAS A SUSPECT!**

"But . . . but . . . I'm good," was all Grumbolt could get out.

"We don't know what you are!" Rex countered. "You might be a monster, a goblin, or an angry puppy!"

"I'm not a monster," Grumbolt said.

"So what are you?" Rex yelled.

Grumbolt had had enough. He leaped at Rex, fists raised!

This was a bad idea, for two reasons:

1. IF YOU ARE TRYING TO PROVE YOU
   ARE GOOD, ATTACKING SOMEONE IS A
   HORRIBLE WAY TO DO IT.
2. REX EVERYTHING WAS WAY STRONGER
   THAN GRUMBOLT.

Rex tapped his shoulder, activating his Rex-in-Effect kick. It knocked Grumbolt right to the ground.

T4-2 rolled between Rex and Grumbolt.

"You both get detention! Rex, go to class. Grumbolt, go to the toy infirmary and have someone look at that rip. You're losing cotton."

A nurse doll was stitching Grumbolt's chin when a Beat-Bot appeared with a note from Commander Hedgehog. It took Grumbolt a while to decode, as the commander was normally left-handed and the left hand in question was currently missing.

CHAPTER THIRTEEN
POLKA DOT MARKS THE SPOT

A depressed Grumbolt sat with his friends outside. "Rex Everything calls me evil and has completely made me mistrust coat racks, and I get in trouble? It's not fair." Grumbolt sighed.

"Ignore it," Micro said. "Concentrate on what matters. Why are you here?"

"To get a kid!" Grumbolt said.

"Exactly." Micro continued. "To get a kid, you need to graduate. To graduate, you need to improve your grades. Maybe you need a tutor?"

"I used to stink at Posing 101," Pepper said. "But I started getting tutored by a bowling trophy. He's done wonders. I've held this exact same pose for almost an hour."

Maybe a tutor was the answer. The only problem was, Grumbolt was struggling in every class. He'd need a *lot* of tutors.

Looking across the campus, over at the Margie Princess Dream Mansion, gave him an idea. He excused himself, ran away from his friends, and left the campus. Grumbolt hurried down the hill and into a residential area called Knickknack Valley Suburbs. There, among the boring dollhouses, was the Mega-Deluxe Margie Princess Dream Tower.

Grumbolt ran up the driveway, past a polka-dot sports car, past a polka-dot minivan, past a polka-dot tank, and past a polka-dot unicorn. He reached the polka-dot door and rang the doorbell. The door opened, and Grumbolt was face-to-face with Margie, the most popular doll in the world.

"Wow, you're world famous, but you answer your own door," Grumbolt said, impressed. "You don't have a bodyguard or a polka-dot attack dog or anything."

"I'm a black belt in five styles of martial arts," Margie said, laughing warmly. "I'm also a superspy and a superhero, so . . ."

She invited Grumbolt in. He sat down in a big polka-dot easy chair as she brought out a plate of chocolate chip cookies, fresh from the Margie Bake Oven.

"How can I help you?" Margie asked.

"I'm a plush at Toy Academy, but I'm not doing well in my classes. I can't do tea parties, I panic at dress-up, and if I ever *do* have to hug, these mismatched arms are gonna blow it," Grumbolt explained. "I need help with **EVERYTHING**! So I thought, find a toy who can **DO EVERYTHING**! You're a baseball champion, you're a scientist, you're a mermaid. If I learn from you, I learn from the best!"

"I wouldn't say I'm the best, per se." Margie laughed. "No, I guess I am. And I would love to help; I love to help everyone. But right now is the *worst* time. I'm about to leave for a supermodel photo shoot. In space. Also, I have to perform a quadruple bypass surgery. Also in space."

"Wow," Grumbolt said. "Must be cool to be great at something."

"Great at everything," Margie corrected him.

A disappointed Grumbolt thanked Margie for her time and slumped to the door.

"You will find your way," Margie said. "Just be yourself."

On the walk back to Toy Academy, Grumbolt thought about what Margie had said: **"JUST BE YOURSELF."**

Good advice. But it's hard to be yourself when you don't know what you are. He was some mystery animal, and that mystery was making him fail out of Toy Academy *and* making him a suspect in the great commander-arm theft.

Maybe that's what Margie was getting at. Maybe that was the solution.

Grumbolt had to figure out exactly what he was.

CHAPTER FOURTEEN
SEW MYSTERIOUS

Micro was very excited to help Grumbolt figure out what he was supposed to be. She was a toy historian, and this mystery was right up her alley. The only clue Grumbolt had was that he was from a pattern by the **U CAN SEW** company.

"That's more than enough information!" Micro proclaimed. "This school has a **HALL OF INSTRUCTION MANUALS**. Every manual, pattern, and booklet for every toy. I'll find your pattern by the end of the day."

Micro went off to the hall, but Grumbolt

couldn't wait. He wanted to figure out what he was for himself. There were many clubs and organizations on campus for every kind of toy, so he decided to join a few to see if any of them felt like a good fit.

The first club meeting he attended was **THE UNITED CATS OF TOY ACADEMY**.

The leader of the group, a fat-cat window-plunger doll, welcomed Grumbolt to the group.

"Question," a black-cat Halloween decoration said. "Are you really a cat? You don't have whiskers or a cat tail."

"The truth is, I'm not sure what I am," Grumbolt said. "But I may be a cat. The first creature I ever met was a cat, and I felt a real connection until she tried to eat me."

"All in favor of letting Grumbolt in on a probationary basis, say meow," Fat-Cat Window-Plunger Doll declared. "All those opposed, please hiss."

The meows had it, and Grumbolt was allowed to stay. But when they began to sing their official club song, things went downhill.

Oh, everyone here's a cat
Everyone here is definitely a cat
Definitely, definitely, definitely
A cat, cat, cat
If there's even the slightest chance that you're not a cat, you should probably leave
Leave right meow
Because this is a club
This is a club
This is a club
For CATS (and cats only)

Grumbolt snuck out the side door. He would not be returning to that club.

Grumbolt tried many more clubs—Toy Dogs of the World, Stuffed Mythological Creatures Anonymous, Future Wind-Up Business Leaders of America (Who Are, Without Question, Rodents)—but none of them seemed like an ideal fit. This day was becoming a total wash. Grumbolt hoped Micro was having better luck.

She was not.

Micro had found the **U CAN SEW** patterns in the Hall of Instruction Manuals, but there was a slight problem. None of them seemed to match Grumbolt exactly.

After hours of research, she had only been able to narrow Grumbolt's species down to "probably not a reptile."

Back at the dorm, she broke the news. "Even if your maker *did* use a pattern," Micro said gently, "maybe she wasn't very good at sewing. A few wrong cuts here, some overstuffing there, she might have veered off-course."

Grumbolt knew Micro might be right. What animal has arms that are two different lengths? And a giant head?

"Maybe . . ." Grumbolt hung his head low. "Maybe I'm not **ANYTHING**."

"I'm sorry, Grumbolt," Micro said. "I really am."

Just then, a familiar figure burst in the door. Grumbolt thought it was Commander Hedgehog at first, but the hot-pink hands were a dead giveaway: It was Bootleg.

"Did you guys hear?" Bootleg said, out of breath. "There's been another robbery! The Evil Toy Academy has stolen Commander Hedgehog's other arm!"

CHAPTER FIFTEEN
THE SOUND OF NO HANDS CLAPPING

That night, Grumbolt couldn't sleep. He felt terrible for Commander Hedgehog. Without those arms, Castle Fort Lair was useless. Not even the Beat-Bots' control pad could be activated without the commander's right arm. These were truly dark times for Toy Academy. If only someone could do something. If only someone could make things right. If only someone could pose as a villain and break into the Evil Toy Academy and get those arms back.

Grumbolt jumped out of bed and ran straight to Micro's dorm room. He banged on the door. A groggy Micro opened it.

"This had better be good," she said, yawning. "I was having a dream that I was on display at the Smithsonian."

"I might be a monster, right?" Grumbolt said.

"This again?" Micro said. "I mean, maybe. But you might also be a gopher."

"I'm saying, I could pass for a monster," Grumbolt explained. "Enough to fool the Evil Toy Academy, anyway . . ."

"Uh, no way," Micro said. "No, that's dangerous. You can't go there all alone."

"So come with me," Grumbolt said. "We can get some temporary paint and make you look evil! The two of us together will find those arms in no time."

Micro thought about it. She wanted to go; she wanted to help her friend. But she couldn't. "I'd have to take my bag off," Micro said sadly. "I can't risk scuffs; that would lower my value."

"Fine," Grumbolt said, determined. "I'll do it myself. Everyone in school wants to know what I am? After tonight, the answer will be simple. I'll be the guy who got Commander Hedgehog's arms back."

CHAPTER SIXTEEN
BURGER TIME

Grumbolt snuck through the campus toward the exit. He had almost successfully scaled the block fence when he heard a scratchy metallic voice behind him. It was OmniBus Squared, and he was even crabbier than usual.

"What are you doing, Grumbolt?" he said. "Are you the thief? I'm the one who recruited you. If you're evil, I'm gonna be *so* fired."

"No! I'm not evil! No, no, sir!" Grumbolt stammered. "But I was going to sneak into the Evil Toy Academy to see if I could find Commander Hedgehog's arms."

Officially, OmniBus Squared could not allow a Toy Academy student to go looking for trouble at the Evil Toy Academy. Unofficially, however, OmniBus loved this idea. He drove Grumbolt right to Mount Skull, the playset that served as the home base for the Evil Toy Academy.

The road leading up to the Evil Toy Academy was littered with multicolored chalk outlines of various dismembered toys. The dark clouds over the playset swirled angrily. Grumbolt could feel the cotton in his belly stir. Maybe this was a bad idea.

"Just act evil and you'll be fine," OmniBus said. "And if you see the Guard Burger, run."

Grumbolt nodded, took a deep breath, and walked over the drawbridge leading to the main gates of Mount Skull. The moat was full of windup alligators chomping hungrily.

As he reached the other side, it hit him: the overwhelming stench of fast food. And then something else hit him square in the back of the head: a French fry.

Grumbolt turned to see the Guard Burger step out of the shadows. The monster was truly a horrific sight to behold: He was made out of the most dangerous pieces of various fast-food toys. The Guard Burger was held together by glue, and powered by rage.

"Where do you think you're going?" the Guard Burger barked, aiming his fry bazooka at Grumbolt.

Grumbolt almost answered politely. Luckily, he caught himself just in the nick of time. To survive the Guard Burger, to get into that school, he needed to act bad. So he imitated the worst toy he knew.

"Move it, loser! I don't have time for you!" Grumbolt yelled in his best Rex Everything voice. "I'm the strongest toy ever!"

"What'd you say to me?" The Guard Burger lunged at Grumbolt, ready to strike.

"You wanna rumble? Let's go." Grumbolt went to tap his own shoulder. "But I gotta say, you don't want a taste of my action feature. I call it the **GRUMBOLT-OF-LIGHTNING**, and it's so powerful they almost discontinued me."

The Guard Burger stopped and thought about this.

"You *do* kind of look like an evil hamster," the Guard Burger said. He stepped out of the way. The gates opened.

"Go on in," the Guard Burger said.

Grumbolt walked right by him, saying, "Thank you, Mr. Guard Burger. No wait, I was just kidding. I don't thank you; I don't thank *anyone*."

He passed through the gates. Grumbolt had made it into the Evil Toy Academy.

CHAPTER SEVENTEEN
BAD APTITUDE

It was the dead of night, so class was in session. Vampire figures, monster trucks, and demons with light-up eyes were hurrying to their evil classes. Grumbolt needed to find the commander's arms and get out as soon as possible. He rushed down the hall, bumping into a long rubber snake wearing glasses and a tie.

"Excuse me," Grumbolt said.

"Random act of politenesssssssss!" the snake hissed. "That's detention for you!"

Grumbolt nodded nervously and ran into the nearest classroom and took a seat. He noticed the teacher immediately glaring at him with cold, black eyes.

"Who are you?" the teacher growled.

"Who are *you*?" Grumbolt responded.

"I'm Dr. Shark-Dentist," he replied. "And I've never seen you before. **INTRUDER!**"

Every student in the classroom jumped out of their seats and aimed their accessories at Grumbolt!

He thought he was done for, when Dr. Shark-Dentist pointed a fin. "Wait a minute! Zandar the Chameleon? Evil Master of Disguise?" Dr. Shark-Dentist's face broke out in a huge, fang-filled smile. "Excellent costume, Zandar! I would have never figured it was you! You look so goofy!"

The students sat back down and Dr. Shark-Dentist went back to writing on the chalkboard. Grumbolt resumed his mission. He turned to the students next to him—a pile of ooze and a skunk with a sword.

"Hey, guys, it's me, Zandar, the evil chameleon. So, either of you ever steal anyone's arms?" Grumbolt asked. "I have; it's cool if you have. Like, did you guys hear someone stole Commander Hedgehog's arms? Isn't that funny? Who was it? I want to congratulate them."

"No one here stole those arms," Dr. Shark-Dentist said. He was clearly eavesdropping (how evil!). "The faculty did some snooping to see if it was a student so we could give them extra credit, but we came up empty-handed. It was an outside job."

Grumbolt had broken into the Evil Toy Academy for nothing. And just as he was about to fake sickness so he could leave . . . the actual Zandar the Chameleon ran in.

"I know, I know! I'm late. I overslept, back off!" Zandar growled. He looked at Grumbolt. "Who's that?"

"Who am I? That is a funny, evil story . . ." was the only thing Grumbolt could muster before he ran out of the room. He tore down the hallway as sirens began to wail.

Students and teachers marched out of the classrooms, accessories raised, ready to fight. Grumbolt burst through the main gates, past the Guard Burger, and down the road.

"How'd it go?" OmniBus asked as he pulled out from behind the plastic rock.

As if to answer, the students and faculty stampeded out of the building behind Grumbolt.

"If we're being honest, it could have gone better," Grumbolt said. He jumped on the back of the bus and they sped down the road, away from the Evil Toy Academy. The evil toys, led by a very angry Chancellor Thornbones, were gaining fast. OmniBus hit the gas and raced toward Toy Academy, dodging lasers, foam torpedoes, and French fries. Grumbolt and the old bus barely made it back home, charging through the main gates and slamming them shut once they passed.

But the Evil Toy Academy wasn't stopping. Chancellor Thornbones smashed through the block walls

THE EVIL STUDENTS HAD INVADED TOY ACADEMY.

CHAPTER EIGHTEEN
SCHOOL'S OUT

"What's this about?" Commander Hedgehog barked. Even with no arms, he was ready to throw down. Thornbones was in for quite the kicking, until he explained that Grumbolt had broken into his school.

"You bet I did!" Grumbolt said. "But only because I wanted the commander's arms back! Uh, quick update, Commander: They do not have the arms."

"If we *did* steal them, we'd do something fun with them," Thornbones declared. "We'd leave riddles or use them to set a trap. But that's neither here nor there; your student invaded MY school, and I can't just let that go."

If the commander didn't do something soon, there was about to be a battle between good and evil right on Toy Academy grounds. As much as it killed him to do so, Commander Hedgehog apologized.

Chancellor Thornbones and his school left Toy Academy, triumphant.

"You brought my archenemy right to my doorstep and endangered everyone here," the commander said to Grumbolt. "You are expelled. I want you off campus. You have one hour to gather your accessories. You too, OmniBus."

And just like that, Grumbolt's stay at Toy Academy was over. All his hopes and dreams of having a kid to call his own were smashed. And it was all his fault.

"They can't kick you out for trying to help the commander!" Micro declared. "The Evil Toy Academy took his arms!"

"No, they didn't," Grumbolt said. "And I still have no idea who did."

"I'm going to continue your investigation," Micro vowed. "I'll snoop around. I'll find the culprit."

"You can't be sneaky in a plastic bag," Grumbolt said bluntly. "And I don't want you to risk getting kicked out. You're going to graduate from Toy Academy and be the best toy in someone's collection."

The two friends tried to hug each other good-bye. Grumbolt could barely wrap his short arm around her large plastic bag.

"I knew I couldn't hug." Grumbolt sighed.

"No," Micro said sadly. "It's the stupid bag."

Grumbolt held up his arms. "No, it's these things. Nothing about me is good."

Bootleg shook Grumbolt's paw and said, "Don't let this get you down. You and I, we're more than everyone thinks we are. Everyone will see that someday."

Grumbolt headed for what was left of the front gates when he felt eight taps on his back. It was Irving Spider-Ring.

"I feel like I failed you as a guidance counselor," Irving said solemnly. "Look, kid, I'm not giving up on you. I'm gonna land you a job in the human world."

True to his word, Irving found Grumbolt a job.

AND IT WAS THE WORST.

CHAPTER NINETEEN
MALL OR NOTHING

The mall Christmas tree had a new ornament on it that year, and a very grumpy new angel.

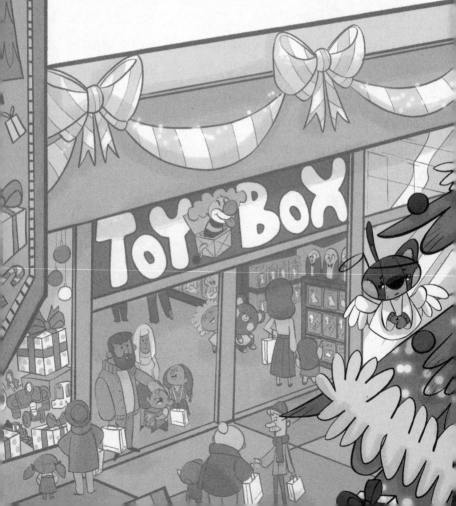

Grumbolt spent his first day watching toys being taken out of the toy store, excited to begin their new lives with their new children. He was happy for them, and at the same time completely heartbroken that he'd never know what having his own kid felt like.

That night, OmniBus left the tree as soon as the humans were gone. Grumbolt unhooked himself from his limb and followed OmniBus into the store.

He was surprised to see OmniBus simply sitting on the floor of aisle eight, staring up at the new model robots. Grumbolt started to leave, assuming the old robot wanted to be left alone. But then, OmniBus started talking.

"I was on the bottom shelf when my kid found me," OmniBus said. "That's the worst shelf, shoe level, but he found me. He used to throw me off the couch, throw me at the dog, throw me off the porch . . . But, man, did he love me."

He turned to Grumbolt and said, "I'm sorry you never got a kid."

"Would have been cool," Grumbolt said. "But what kid is gonna want some mystery animal when they could have a robot or an action figure?"

"Eh, robots can be one of two things. Kid takes us home, plays with us in robot mode. Gets bored, transforms us into a vehicle. That's it, there are no other options. Action figures got it worse; they're *one* thing. But no one knows what the heck you are. *You* don't know who you are. So if you're not anything . . . you can *be* anything. Anything you want." OmniBus paused. "Well, you *coulda* been anything. Before we got kicked out. But now, it's over for us."

Grumbolt stood up. "If we have to be a Christmas ornament and a weird robot angel, then let's try to be the best Christmas ornament and weird robot angel ever. Are you with me?"

Grumbolt ripped off his Christmas mitten and put his paw out for OmniBus to shake.

OmniBus did not take it.

"Clean your paw, Grumbolt," he said. "You've got some pink on it."

OmniBus was right; he had spots of hot-pink paint on his paw.

"Must have come from Bootleg when we shook," Grumbolt said. "But why would his paint be coming off?"

"Maybe he got scuffed and needed a touch-up." OmniBus shrugged.

But this wasn't a touch-up, this was a *lot* of paint.

And then the truth hit Grumbolt like a pillow to the face.

"OmniBus, what if Bootleg painted his arms because they *weren't* his arms?" Grumbolt said. "What if he stole the commander's arms and painted them pink to look like his?"

"Why would he do that?" OmniBus asked.

"The commander's arms were better made, they could hold more things . . ." Grumbolt thought about it further and started to worry. "Those arms unlock all sorts of secrets in the most powerful playset in the Toy World. He'd have full control of Castle Fort Lair. So many weapons—"

"And," OmniBus said, "maybe, possibly, a sno-cone maker. Kid, we gotta get back to school."

Grumbolt and OmniBus raced to the discount section. On the floor was another Warp Zone playset, the key to getting back to the Toy World. But they had been banned from ever returning, and Sven, Guardian of the Warp Zone, was not letting them through.

"This is a matter of life and death, Sven!" Grumbolt yelled. Sven wasn't having any of it.

"I'm gonna knock him down with one of my foam missiles," OmniBus said.

But Grumbolt realized there was another way. "Play some music on your radio," he told OmniBus. "Something with violins, pianos, and rain, and maybe humpback whales singing."

"That sounds boring," OmniBus shot back.

"Exactly," Grumbolt whispered. "I'm gonna tell Sven a bedtime story."

OmniBus found a radio station (RAIN 105: Music Your Great-Great-Grandparents Would Love) that was playing a soft, calming tune.

"Excellent, now put your hands over your ears," Grumbolt instructed. OmniBus did.

"Sven," Grumbolt said. "Did you ever hear the story of the sheep and the pillow and the warm milk?"

Sven had NOT heard of that story, because up until that point, such a story didn't exist. Grumbolt was making it up as he went along, and he was telling it in his best imitation of Professor Cupcake Pillow's soft, melodic voice.

"Once upon a time, a sheep, his best friend pillow, and a glass of warm milk went on an adventure. Not TOO much of an adventure, nothing to get excited about, a mellow adventure involving a good, long nap…"

Sven was out.

"Wow," OmniBus said. "You really pay attention in class."

"I try," Grumbolt said.

OmniBus activated the Warp Zone playset, transformed into a bus (three minutes, new record), and took Grumbolt through.

What was waiting for them was the stuff of toy nightmares.

CHAPTER TWENTY
KICK BOTS

There were Beat-Bots everywhere. The plastic robot army had swarmed Toy World's residential area. They had seized the countryside. And they had completely taken over both schools. Hot-pink flags waved over everything the robots had taken down.

"That's Bootleg's signature color! So he *is* behind this! I'm finally right about something and it's **THIS**!" Grumbolt said. "We have to bring the Beat-Bots down!"

"Good luck. They're programmed to analyze any opponent and find their weakness in seconds," OmniBus reminded Grumbolt.

Grumbolt and OmniBus watched as the Guard Burger barreled toward a herd of Beat-Bots, who scanned him.

SPECIES: BURGER CREATURE
WEAKNESS: FLAME BROILING

A Beat-Bot rolled up with a Margie Grill and turned it on. The Guard Burger gasped and surrendered. He knew he was beaten.

Grumbolt looked toward Toy Academy and saw Rex Everything running away from campus. Beat-Bots were in hot pursuit. Rex activated his **REX-IN-EFFECT** kick and knocked a few away. Then the Beat-Bots scanned him.

SPECIES: ARMY MAN
WEAKNESS: SHEER NUMBERS

The Beat-Bots began piling on Rex. He tapped his shoulder to activate his kick. But the tiny robots swarmed him and held the leg down.

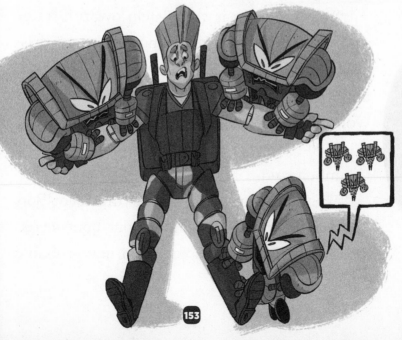

Rex was a bully, but Grumbolt couldn't sit back and let him be taken. He ran toward the melee, yelling, "Kick with your other leg, Rex!"

"No way!" Rex yelled. "That's not my action feature!"

"Exactly! They'll never see it coming!" Grumbolt exclaimed.

Rex sighed and kicked with his other leg. **WHAM!** One Beat-Bot went flying back! **WHAM!** Another! Grumbolt's plan was working. Soon Rex had kicked himself free of the Beat-Bots. He hurried over to Grumbolt and OmniBus.

"Toy Academy is completely overrun!" Rex said. "Bootleg has taken almost everyone prisoner, including the commander! I barely got out alive! Let's find a Warp Zone and get out of Toy World before it's too late!"

"No. Bootleg has to be stopped," Grumbolt said.

"We can't go back! There are Beat-Bots **EVERYWHERE**. They can figure out your weakness in seconds," Rex said. "And you probably

have, like, eighty weaknesses." Rex thought
about what he'd said, and quickly mumbled,
"No offense."

"Actually, Rex," Grumbolt said, "you just
gave me an idea."

CHAPTER TWENTY-ONE
ARMED AND DANGEROUS

On the fifth floor of Castle Fort Lair, Beat-Bots moved a Margie Bake Oven into place.

"Beat-Bots, throw the commander in!" Bootleg exclaimed.

The Beat-Bots obeyed their new master and tossed Commander Hedgehog into the oven. Bootleg turned the dial, activating the oven's powerful heat lamp.

"Once you're melted, I'll take over. I'll be a better Commander Hedgehog then you ever were," Bootleg sneered. "Do you know that I've already taken down Thornbones's school?"

"Bootleg, enough!" Salt pleaded, climbing up the stairs.

"Don't call me that!" Bootleg yelled, turning toward the condiment dispenser. "My name is **COMMANDANT HEDGEPIG**! I have seized control of the school, I have vanquished the Evil Toy Academy, and you are no match for the likes of me!"

But Salt wasn't there to fight Bootleg. He simply wanted to distract him so Pepper could sneak in and free Commander Hedgehog. She tiptoed to the oven and slowly pulled the door open.

It made a tiny CLICK.

Which Bootleg heard immediately.

"Nice try!" Bootleg yelled as he grabbed Castle Fort Lair's Trubble-Bubble-Maker. He waved his stolen hands over the gun, unlocking it, then aimed it at Pepper and fired. Salt bravely dove in front of his sister to shield her from the soapy onslaught—but both got trapped in a thick pink bubble! Pepper kicked but couldn't break the bubble. Salt tried next; he punched with his ceramic fist, but the bubble was too durable.

Bootleg strutted back to the Margie Bake Oven and used his new hands to turn up the heat.

CHAPTER TWENTY-TWO
THE FALL OF MICRO

Micro and a handful of other students watched from the dorm roof as Grumbolt snuck back onto campus. He was headed right for Castle Fort Lair, completely unaware that there was a quartet of Beat-Bots closing in. Micro tried yelling to Grumbolt, but he couldn't hear her.

"We have to do something!" Micro said to the group. But nobody was moving. Even if they wanted to help, the dorms were super-high. If they jumped, the fall would certainly break them. And Paper Dave had thrown the ladder *and* the slide off the playset so no Beat-Bots could climb up.

"My bad." Paper Dave shrugged. "We're stuck up here."

They watched as the Beat-Bots began to chase Grumbolt, who ran from them as fast as he could. He was doing his best, moving too fast to be scanned, but the Bots were quickly gaining.

GRUMBOLT WAS DONE FOR.

Micro couldn't bear to watch any more. She turned away . . .

. . . reached down

. . . and unzipped the bottom of her protective bag.

With shaking hands, Micro lifted the bag over her head and **JUMPED OFF** the roof.

The bag served as a parachute, slowing her fall. Adjusting for wind, Micro was able to land directly next to Grumbolt. She kicked a Beat-Bot off her friend, and before any of them had a chance to retaliate, she punched one, karate chopped a second, and threw the third into a plastic bush.

"Micro! You're out of the bag!" Grumbolt said, astonished. "But, your value—"

"I'VE NEVER FELT MORE VALUABLE!" Micro shouted. "Nobody puts Micro on a shelf! I want to live!"

Beat-Bot reinforcements heard the ruckus and were headed their way.

"I'll head them off!" Micro said. "Climb up Castle Fort Lair's slide, it'll take you right to Bootleg."

"But slides are for sliding *down*," Grumbolt said.

"Sometimes you gotta break the rules," Micro said. "And be careful of all the trapdoors. If you see a part of the floor that is a **DIFFERENT COLOR** than the rest, step over it! Good luck!"

She hugged Grumbolt. He returned it.

"See, you can hug, Grumbolt," Micro said. "In fact, you're great at it."

Micro ran toward the Beat-Bots. "Now, go save the commander!"

Grumbolt began climbing up the slide.

CHAPTER TWENTY-THREE
PLAYTIME BEGINS

The commander could feel his leg joints start to loosen under the heat of the Margie Bake Oven. Pepper and Salt took turns kicking and punching the bubble, but they couldn't break through the impressively thick, soapy shell.

"Commander," Bootleg said, "before you become a pile of gooey plastic, do you mind telling me just how many secrets this place has? I mean, does it *really* have a sno-cone maker?"

The commander didn't say a word.

"Fine," Bootleg growled, "if you won't talk, we don't need you around."

He went to turn the dial one more time—

—and that's when Grumbolt tumbled in through the window.

"Grumbolt?" Bootleg couldn't believe it. He reached out a hot-pink hand . . .

. . . AND
HELPED
GRUMBOLT UP.

"What do you think?" Bootleg said. "Everyone counted us out! They said I was a rip-off and you were some worthless mystery doll. But I overthrew Toy Academy! And you . . . well, you haven't done anything good yet, but you can be my number two if you want."

"No," Grumbolt declared. "Commandant Hedgepig, this is over."

"First of all, thank you for calling me by my real name," Bootleg said. "Second, no. It's not over. The Beat-Bots are under my control, and the commander is melting. There are no toys left to stop me!"

Grumbolt raised his mismatched arms and made two fists. **"THERE'S ME."**

The Beat-Bots surrounded Grumbolt. There were at least fifty encircling him, ready to attack.

"Come on, then," Grumbolt said. "Let's do this."

They did a quick scan.

SPECIES: UNKNOWN

The robots froze. They tried another scan.

SPECIES: UNKNOWN

One of the Beat-Bots moved in closer, examining Grumbolt head to toe, and then inquired:

WHAT. ARE. YOU.

Grumbolt smiled. "You tell me."

They began searching their files, running through all the possibilities. The robots, like everyone else Grumbolt had met, like Grumbolt himself, had no idea what Grumbolt was.

So they didn't have the slightest clue how to stop him.

Grumbolt took a paw and gently tapped the nearest robot. It fell, taking down the one behind it and the one behind it and the one behind it. Every single robot was defeated in seconds, and Grumbolt didn't throw a single punch.

Only Bootleg stood between Grumbolt and Commander Hedgehog.

"Oh, big deal, your secret weapon is that you were poorly made?" Bootleg yelled. "I was forged in a factory! By a state-of-the-art machine! I'm made from rubber and resin and plastic! What are YOU made from?"

"It's not what you're made from," Grumbolt said, calmly walking toward Bootleg. "IT'S WHAT YOU'RE MADE OF."

Bootleg was not impressed. He waved his stolen arm over a giant red button, activating it.

"What does that do?" Grumbolt asked.

"I have no idea." Bootleg shrugged. "It was the closest one."

Red ice began shooting out of a rubber nozzle, coating the floor.

Bootleg had discovered Castle Fort Lair's sno-cone maker.

"No way!" Bootleg exclaimed.

"It does have one!" Grumbolt said. "Micro is gonna freak!"

Bootleg aimed the nozzle toward Grumbolt, coating the floor around him in a sheet of slippery, cherry-flavored ice. He walked back to the oven and put his hands on the dial.

"Let's go maximum power, shall we?" Bootleg said.

Grumbolt tried to walk across the floor, but it was too slippery.

Salt and Pepper continued taking turns punching and kicking their bubble, to no avail. Then Pepper had an idea. "Salt, kick together, in unison!"

On the count of three, Salt and Pepper kicked through the bubble, bursting it in a fantastic explosion of water and suds. They fell to the floor, cracking their legs and chipping their paint.

Pepper staggered to her feet. She grabbed her brother by the ankles and spun him upside down.

"What are you doing?" Salt yelped.

Pepper shook her brother vigorously, coating the cherry ice in salt. The ice began to melt, immediately becoming less slippery. Grumbolt could now safely run across! He barreled toward Bootleg.

"My new hands can hold more than pans and plungers." Bootleg swung the commander's space axe. "And I've been trained in accessory combat!"

"Well, I took a semester of pillow fighting," Grumbolt shot back.

"I've seen you in class!" Bootleg yelled. "You stink at pillow fighting!"

It was true. Grumbolt's arms were uneven, which made it difficult to effectively swing the pillow. But it turned out he'd never needed to use his arms to pillow fight—or even a pillow.

He head-butted Bootleg with his massive, overstuffed head. Bootleg staggered back and tried to retaliate. But before he could do anything, Grumbolt head-butted him again. And again. And again.

Bootleg was weakened but not out.

When Grumbolt lowered his head again, he saw a piece of the floor that was a slightly darker shade than the rest. As Bootleg ran at him, he braced himself . . .

. . . and delivered one last, perfectly positioned head-butt.

Bootleg staggered back, stepping on the piece of differently colored floor—one of Castle Fort Lair's many **TRAPDOORS**.

Bootleg fell through, into a plastic jail cell. "Part pillow," Bootleg said in awe, looking up at Grumbolt. "You are part pillow."

"Yep," Grumbolt said. "Part pillow, and some other parts I haven't figured out yet."

Bootleg sighed. He had been beaten.

Grumbolt walked over to the Margie Bake Oven and pulled the plug. He had saved Commander Hedgehog, his friends, and Toy Academy itself.

CHAPTER TWENTY-FOUR

BACK TO SCHOOL

Grumbolt, Salt, and Pepper helped Commander Hedgehog out of the oven. He thanked them, checked to see if anything important had melted, and then took his arms back.

The next day, **COMMANDER HEDGEHOG** had a lukewarm bath and treated himself to a new paint job.

OMNIBUS SQUARED's time as talent scout, transportation, and substitute gym teacher was over. Instead, Commander Hedgehog gave OmniBus a new job: head of security at Toy Academy.

OmniBus felt like a hero again, and it felt wonderful. (And the plushes were extremely relieved he wasn't their gym teacher anymore.)

BOOTLEG was immediately expelled. But don't be too sad for him.

TODAY'S LESSON: Plotting a Successf
Revenge !!!

1) Find accomplices with similar interests.
2) Go BIGGER!
3) Use better accesso
4) Bide your time, STR at the right moment
5) Destroy Hero's allie
6) CHEAT!!!

REX didn't learn anything this whole adventure, except that he should kick with both legs.

MICRO was now permanently out of her protective bag and had never felt better.

GRUMBOLT had proven how much he had learned from his classes. His ability to play pretend allowed him to sneak into the Evil Toy Academy. His talent for soothing someone to sleep was on full display when he made Sven, Guardian of the Warp Zone, take a nap. And his pillow-fighting technique was the stuff of legend. This, plus the fact that he saved the school and everyone in it, meant that he was allowed back at Toy Academy.

"Are you excited to resume classes on Monday?" Pepper asked her friends.

"I don't know what my classes will be," Micro said, pointing to her scratches. "I'm clearly not a collectible anymore."

"It's obvious. You kick butt. You're an action figure," Grumbolt replied. "I think we both are. I'm gonna ask to change my major, too."

"You're stuffed with cotton and you're huggable," Pepper argued. "Grumbolt, I'm pretty sure you're a plush."

Grumbolt smiled.

"I'm not sure what I am," he said to his friends. "I'm not sure what I'll be. And that's okay."

THE END

CLASSES RESUME SOON

TOY ACADEMY

BOOK 2: READY FOR ACTION

BRIAN LYNCH is a screenwriter whose work includes the movies *The Secret Life of Pets*, *Minions*, *Puss in Boots*, and *Hop*. He has also written the comic books *Monster Motors*, *Bill & Ted's Most Triumphant Return*, *Spike*, and *Angel: After the Fall*. He currently lives in Los Angeles with his wife and son. He firmly believes that the greatest toy is either an Adventure People Daredevil Skydiver or Shipwreck from G.I. Joe.

EDWARDIAN TAYLOR works as a freelance visual development artist for mobile games, TV, films, and commercials in Dallas, Texas. He is also the illustrator of the picture books *Race!*, written by Sue Douglass Fliess, and *It's Not Jack and the Beanstalk*, written by Josh Funk. Learn more about him at www.edwardiantaylor.com and follow him on Twitter, Instagram and Tumblr @edwardiantaylor.

31901062462520